★★★ DEVIL'S DUE PUBLISHING PRESENTS ★★★
A RYAN SCHIFRIN PRODUCTION

SPOOKS ™

STORY BY

R.A. SALVATORE, GENO SALVATORE, AND RYAN SCHIFRIN

WRITTEN BY

RYAN SCHIFRIN AND LARRY HAMA

PENCILS & INKS BY

ADAM ARCHER

COLORED BY

JOHNNY RENCH

LETTERED BY

BRIAN J. CROWLEY

EDITED BY:

STEPHEN CHRISTY

ASSISTANT EDITOR

CODY DEMATTEIS

DESIGN

SEAN K. DOVE

PRODUCTION

SAM WELLS

SPOOKS BASED ON AN ORIGINAL CONCEPT BY

RYAN SCHIFRIN AND DANIEL ALTER

WWW.SPOOKSTHECOMIC.COM

DEVIL'S DUE PUBLISHING:
President JOSH BLAYLOCK
C.E.O. PJ BICKETT
Assistant Publisher SAM WELLS
Art Director SEAN DOVE
Marketing Manager BRIAN WARMOTH
Senior Editor MIKE O'SULLIVAN
I.P. Development STEPHEN CHRISTY
Editorial Assistance CODY DEMATTEIS
Staff Illustrator TIM SEELEY
Staff Illustrator MIKE BEAR
Office Assistance NORA HICKEY
Manager of Finance DEBBIE DAVIS

SPOOKS Vol 1. JUNE, 2008.

ISBN-13: 978-1-934692-01-1
ISBN 10: 1-934692-01-8

Published by Devil's Due Publishing, Inc. Office of publication 3759 N. Ravenswood Ave. #230, Chicago, IL 60613.

For Ad Sales, please contact adsales@devilsdue.net

www.devilsdue.net

- INTRODUCTION -

Monsters. Can't live with 'em. Can't live without 'em. One way or another they'll always be with us... or within us!

I met my first monster at the age of 5. My Dad woke me up late one night and said there was something on television I really should see. It turned out to be James Whale's *Frankenstein* and I think, for me, it was love at first sight. I was hooked on monsters from that day on. Fascinated and terrified by them in equal measure. It was a bonus for me that my Dad also loved monsters, and he's an excellent artist with a vivid imagination, so when we weren't watching old Universal horror movies or *Doctor Who*, he could always whistle up some new abomination with a pencil and piece of paper. I had monsters on tap!

Through movies, television, art and books, monsters kept their grip on my imagination. I remember being so disappointed when the *Hound of the Baskervilles* turned out to be just a hound, and not some terrible hell-dog with burning red eyes, hot foul breath and gleaming white fangs. Given the choice, I would always prefer the monster over reality. When it came to making my first feature film, *Dog Soldiers*, the same rule applied, it just had to be a monster movie, so I chose my favourite monster of all – the WEREWOLF!

The old one's are still the best, and *SPOOKS* takes the time-honoured tradition of soldiers vs monsters and turns it all the way up to 11. The Department of Supernatural Defense are professional monster killers, with all the latest hi-tech hardware, and they're up against the best of the best – werewolves, vampires, zombies, witches, even the headless horseman himself! It's a total monster mash and I love the brutality of it all. *SPOOKS* continues this long standing tradition in great style with relentless energy, bloody action, but most of all, a real sense of fun and love of the genre. These comics are a hell of a ride!

Neil Marshall

(WRITER/DIRECTOR OF DOG SOLDIERS, THE DESCENT & DOOMSDAY

MISSION STATEMENT OF THE
DEPARTMENT OF SUPERNATURAL DEFENSE

The United States Department of Supernatral Defense (DOSD) recruits, trains, arms and deploys specially trained forces based within the nation's borders in support of national security and defense strategies. To accomplish this, they provide relevant and ready support to commanders whose mission is to keep the country free of supernatural enemies, whether their origins are domestic, international, or otherworldly.

OMNIA MONSTRA DELENDA SUNT

LOOKS LIKE WE *BOTH* LOSE...

...SOON YOU'LL BE ONE OF *US!*

HATE TO BURST YOUR BUBBLE SON, BUT THE WEREWOLF VIRUS DOESN'T AFFECT ME. THAT'S WHY I GOT PICKED TO SLAP A MUZZLE ON YA.

SCRATCH ONE DIRT-BAG SHAPE-SHIFTER...

...LOOKS LIKE THE SAME EUROPEAN STRAIN AS THE OTHERS.

THAT'S WHAT I WAS AFRAID OF. HOW MANY CIVILIANS WERE INFECTED?

TWO...

...AND LOTS OF WITNESSES TO CONVINCE IT WAS NOTHING MORE THAN A RABID DOG...

RELAX. ZACH'S ONE OF THE LUCKY .001% OF THE POPULATION THAT'S IMMUNE TO LYCANTHROPY.

SIR... ABOUT RAMIREZ... HE'S BEEN BITTEN...

FRANK, WE'VE GOT A SITUATION UP IN MASSACHUSETTS... BRAVO TEAM IS ON THE SCENE.

HIT THE LIGHTS!

THIS IS THE U.S. COAST GUARD. YOU ARE IN VIOLATION OF OUR NATIONAL WATERS! PREPARE TO BE BOARDED

U.S. COAST GUARD

THIS IS WEIRD, CHIEF- WHERE'S THE CREW OF THIS TUB--?

U.S.C.G

SMASH

GRARGH!

WHAT THE--?

DON'T JUST STAND THERE, SHOOT HIM!

HAVE WE ARRIVED ALREADY, ZERGUNHEIM?

AH, AMERICA! THE LAND OF *PLENTY!*

NOW WHERE MIGHT WE FIND SOME SUSTENANCE?

"...I'M SIMPLY STARVED!"

AM I WARM?

YOUR POWERS OF DEDUCTION SEEM TO BE WORKING JUST FINE... YOU TELL ME.

JUST GIVE ME A NAME.

SHE WAS MY FORMER APPRENTICE.

AND LOVER?

A GENTLEMAN NEVER TELLS. HER REAL NAME JUST MIGHT BE PATIENCE VAN ANDERS. SHE'S MORE THAN YOU CAN HANDLE, FRANK. SHE BITES.

ENJOY THE REST OF ETERNITY.

YOU THINK LUCIEN WAS TELLING THE TRUTH?

RULE 13: NEVER TRUST A WARLOCK.

GRRRRRRR

BARK! BARK!

GENTLEMEN... WE HAVE A SITUATION.

AT 0400 HOURS, AN UNKNOWN SHIP APPEARED OFF THE COAST OF NEW ORLEANS. THE COAST GUARD ATTEMPTED TO INTERCEPT-- WE'RE STILL SIFTING THROUGH THE WRECKAGE.

THERE WERE PUNCTURE WOUNDS ON THE THROATS OF THE RECOVERED BODIES. WE ALL KNOW WHAT THAT MEANS.

THE BLOOD SUCKERS CAN'T HAVE GOTTEN FAR, AND WILL HAVE GONE TO GROUND AT DAYBREAK. WE HAVE MAPS OF LIKELY NESTING PLACES.

SO WE'LL BE SENDING IN THREE TACTICAL TEAMS TO SET UP SURVEILLANCE-- RADAR AND INFRARED-- UNDEAD DETECTION ARRAYS-- THE WORKS.

WE'LL NAIL THEIR PUTRID HEARTS TO THE WALL.

YOU SURE DO ENJOY KILLING MONSTERS. JUST LIKE THOSE COLD-BLOODED ASSASSINS ON OMEGA TEAM.

DAMN STRAIGHT. WE'RE GOOD, THEY'RE EVIL... NICE AND SIMPLE. DADDY LETTING YOU GO ON THIS MISSION?

SOMEONE HAS TO WATCH YOUR ASS.

I LIKE IT WHEN YOU TALK DIRTY TO ME.

THAT'S YOUR BEST ATTEMPT AT FLIRTING DON JUAN?

MOI? HIT ON THE BOSS'S DAUGHTER? NEVER.

SPEAKING OF WHICH... BE RIGHT BACK...

IT'S ALMOST SUNDOWN, I WANT THOSE PASSIVE ARRAYS IN PLACE NOW!

WE GOT A HIT, STATION FOUR!

OKAY PEOPLE, LET'S MOVE!

HEY, ZACH!

GOOD LU-

SIR, ARE YOU OKAY?

I'M FINE... I'VE SEEN HIM! THE ALL-HEAD-HIGH VAMPIRE HIMSELF! BIGGS, I WAS RIGHT, HE'S THE ONE... THE ONE I'VE BEEN LOOKING FOR.

THIS IS ALPHA TEAM TO BASE. WE'VE LOCATED FRANK, AND NEED EXTRACTION.

OKAY... THERE'S SOMETHING YOU'RE NOT TELLING ME.

EXCUSE ME?

THAT VAMPIRE SAID YOU HAD WITCH BLOOD IN YOU...

NO ONE KNOWS... EXCEPT MY DAD AND BIGGS.

KNOWS WHAT?

I'M... HALF-WITCH.

YOUR MOTHER WAS A WITCH?

SHE WAS A *MONSTER.* FRANK KILLED HER WHEN I WAS AN INFANT-- AFTERWARD, HE DISCOVERED ME NEARBY, WRAPPED IN A BLANKET.

I PROMISED HIM I WOULD NEVER TELL ANYONE ABOUT MY BLOOD-LINE.

SO HE ADOPTED YOU...

HEY... YOUR SECRET IS SAFE WITH ME.

ZACH...NICE WORK. NOW GET YOUR HANDS OFF MY DAUGHTER.

YOU HEARD THE MAN!

FIND THE BACK DOOR TO THIS DUMP!

FALL BACK IN BOUNDING OVERWATCH. ME AND FRANK ARE *COVERING!*

TRY THAT DOOR AT THE END OF THE CORRIDOR–

WE MAY HAVE A PROBLEM.

RAAAR!

CRASH!

PULL OVER!

STEP OUT OF THE VEHICLE. NICE AND SLOW!

YOUR MANIFEST SAYS TRACTOR PARTS... LET'S SEE 'EM!

SURE THING OFFICER.

RIGHT THIS WAY...

ZACH, STEP ON IT!

WHAT DO YOU WANT FROM 584CCS CONVERTED TO *DIESEL?*

SHE'S GAINING ON US!

OH YEAH? LET'S SEE HER KEEP UP WITH--

--THIS!

NOW, WE'VE HAD IT...

NO! THEY'RE ALL *AMERICAN* SOLDIERS...

SCREECH

STOP! LISTEN TO ME! **WE'RE** NOT YOUR ENEMIES!

SHE'S THE ONE YOU SHOULD BE FIGHTING! YOU GOTTA RESIST HER SPELL! REMEMBER WHO YOU ARE!

PATHETIC HUMANS! YOU HAVE NOWHERE LEFT TO RUN!

NOW I'LL ADD YOUR CORPSES TO MY ARMY OF THE UNDEAD!

WE'RE FOOT-SLOGGING OD WEARIN' UNDERPAID UNDER-APPRECIATED NO-FRILLS COMPLAININ'-ABOUT-THE-CHOW G.I. ISSUE GRUNTS... *JUST LIKE YOU USED TO BE.*

ARE YOU WITH US...

...OR WITH **HER?**

LIVE

BREAKING NEWS! A TWENTY BLOCK RADIUS AROUND THE [HOS]PITAL HAS BEEN CLOSED OFF FROM THE PUBLIC. [W]E'RE BEING TOLD THAT [MILI]TARY MANEUVERS HAVE [C]LOSED THE MEMORIAL BRIDGE AS WELL.

BREAKING NEWS - Washington D.C. - KYZW

LIVE

ARLINGTON NATIONAL CEMETERY HAS ALSO BEEN CLOSED, IN WHAT AUTHORITIES ARE SAYING IS NOTHING MORE THAN AN EMERGENCY PREPAREDNESS DRILL.

BREAKING NEWS - Arlington Closed - KYZW

LIVE

THIS CONTRADICTS REPORTS OF A STRANGE COMMOTION AT THE LINCOLN MEMORIAL...

BREAKING NEWS - Washington D.C. - KYZW

AND THE SPIN MACHINE GOES TO WORK. THE REMAINING BATS AND FURBALLS HAVE FLED. AS FAR AS THE PUBLIC IS CONCERNED, THIS NEVER HAPPENED...

OH, BY THE WAY, YOU DID GOOD.

THANK YOU SIR.

STILL NO WORD FROM MY FATHER. HAVE A BAD FEELING THAT- THAT...

DON'T EVEN THINK IT. WE'VE GOT THREE TEAMS LOOKING FOR HIM RIGHT NOW.

THEY FOUND WHAT'S LEFT OF VLAD... YOUR FATHER WON, HE GOT HIS REVENGE... DON'T WORRY, WE'LL FIND HIM.

BUT WHAT IF HE'S HURT SOMEWHERE, WE SHOULD BE OUT THERE HELPING...

TRUST ME...

I'M SURE HE'S OKAY...

ZACH RAMIREZ

CODE NAME: None
REAL NAME: Zach Ramirez
AGE: 30
PLACE OF BIRTH: Canton, Ohio
SPECIALTY: Reconnaissance
RANK: E-5

Highly skilled tracker and recon scout. Qualified for Army Marksmanship Team, but never competed.

The subject was a highly motivated soldier. After graduating from Ranger School, Zach took his first deployment in Afghanistan where his resourcefulness and leadership capabilities were first noted. Upon returning stateside, he applied to and was accepted at the exclusive Reconnaissance and Surveillance School, graduating at the top of his class. He redeployed to Iraq, where an incident involving several dead civilians at a border checkpoint left Zach disillusioned (and suffering from post-traumatic stress disorder.) He put in for Sniper School to escape. As a qualified sniper with a Ranger tab and Recon badge, he went straight back to Afghanistan, where he felt he could have more impact.

Although the military record is still classified, it is believed that Zach was on a secret mission deep in the Hindu Kush mountains when his team ran into a terrorist cell comprised entirely of werewolves. After a fierce firefight, which degraded to a moonlit brawl with knives, teeth and bare hands, Zach defeated the werewolves by reducing them to bodily elements that were too small to keep fighting. He was the sole survivor, and severely wounded, but managed to make his way back to friendly territory, fighting off insurgents all the way. It was the psychological report filed by the Army doctor who treated him that alerted SPOOKS and led to his recruitment.

"Subject has created a complex delusion to cover his guilt and pain at losing the other members of his team. He believes that they were all killed by werewolves. Working within the logic of his delusion, I asked him why he hadn't turned into a werewolf himself, having been bitten by them repeatedly. He had no explanation and became extremely agitated."

Psychological report by Major (RESTRICTED) US Army Medical Corps.

The subject has shown great initiative and leadership ability as one of the new hard-chargers in the front line of the SPOOKS offensive. Being one of .0001% of humans who are immune werewolf bites is a big plus as well. He credits being part of the team with having instilled in him a new resolve and a feeling of worth at a time when his spirits were at low ebb.

FRANK

CODE NAME: The Chief
REAL NAME: (CLASSIFIED)
AGE: 50+
PLACE OF BIRTH: (CLASSIFIED)
SPECIALTY: (CLASSIFIED)
RANK: (CLASSIFIED)

All the Chief's qualifications are classified TOP SECRET. (He is known to have a weakness SOS (creamed chipped beef on toast with grits and eggs.)

A former US Navy SEAL, the Chief left the service to become a professor of comparative religions at a European university, where he remained until his entire family was slaughtered by a creature called "the All-High Head Vampire Himself". He utilized his military experience and his academic propensity towards research to become a ruthless and highly effective monster hunter. He sought the vampire for years, to no avail. In the aftermath of terminating a particularly odious witch, he discovered a baby girl whom he assumed had been abducted for some vile rite. The Chief adopted the girl, who later proved to have magical abilities of her own, indicating that she may have been the witch's actual child.

The Chief was recruited by SPOOKS when the branch was first established (date classified), and he was the top covert field agent until he was wounded in the line of duty. He was shifted to administrative duties and rose to command the unit. He is the final authority in the chain of command, directing all SPOOKS operations from a silver-shielded secret headquarters under hallowed ground at the Washington Monument. His orders can only be countermanded by the President of the United States.

The Chief has been running SPOOKS for longer than anyone else currently on the team can remember. His transfer to a desk job from the field was definitely not voluntary.

All this has resulted in the Chief having a disposition inadequately described as being "ornery," or as Sgt. Gunny Biggs puts it, "10 on the rabid pit-bull scale."

"I take no guff, and I cut no slack. Any swinging Richard who falls in on MY deck had better have their gear squared, their attitude adjusted, and their bullets covered in fresh garlic."

"I've come to think that all of philosophy can be summed up in one sentence. 'There are good-guys and there are monsters, and the job of the good-guys is to kill the monsters."

FELICIA

CODE NAME: Felicia
REAL NAME: (CLASSIFIED)
AGE: Approximately 24
PLACE OF BIRTH: (CLASSIFIED)
SPECIALTY: Forensics
RANK: (CLASSIFIED)

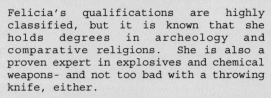

Felicia's qualifications are highly classified, but it is known that she holds degrees in archeology and comparative religions. She is also a proven expert in explosives and chemical weapons- and not too bad with a throwing knife, either.

The Chief's adopted daughter, Felicia is at least half-witch (what the other half is, is anybody's guess.) The SPOOKS psychological unit has raised questions about possible issues she may have concerning the Chief's responsibility in her mother's death, but an internal review board has given her a clean bill of health. She is the forensic tech of the team, as well as the in-the-field font of all knowledge magical, vampiric and lycanthropic. They can also count on her to defuse bombs and stop any infernal device that is ticking…

Beautiful in a gothic way, she is athletic, physically strong, and fast with the sharp repartee. Her sarcastic wit is legendary within SPOOKS and she never passes up the opportunity to let fly with a zinger, even at the most inappropriate times. Her magical powers are somewhat limited (especially in comparison with the opposition) but they are useful nonetheless. She has rudimentary teleki-netic abilities in the moving pencils range, and she has the more advanced ability to dampen the magic around her, neutralizing lower-end spells. Her most valuable ability is being able to see the past by physically touching objects with strong links to a traumatic event.

"You look like something the cat dragged in after a Salem witch barbecue."

"You call that a grenade? THIS is a GRENADE."

"You might be half-way good-looking after a couple of make-overs and a face-transplant."

SGT. BIGGS

CODE NAME: Gunny
REAL NAME: (CLASSIFIED)
AGE: 35
PLACE OF BIRTH: Compton, CA
SPECIALTY:
RANK: E-9

Qualified expert in rifle, pistol, three martial arts and two disciplines involving edged weapons. He is proficient in Arabic, Farsi, Urdu and Swahili, as well as merely conversant in Russian, Spanish, French, Mandarin and Pashto. Can do quadratic equations in his head.

One of the youngest Marines to attain the rank of Master Gunnery Sergeant, Gunny Biggs was well known in the that most elite fraternity of hard men known as the Recon Marines as "Max Salty." In the mid-'90s he was on detached assignment in the former Yugoslavia, leading a special operations unit with the NATO peacekeepers, when his team engaged a unit of paramilitaries with superhuman powers and a taste for drinking blood. Biggs, and two others were the only ones of team to survive the fight. Of the two others, one cut his own throat, and the other is locked in a "quiet room" at a restricted mental facility.

Biggs was transferred "sideways" and as far as his official records are concerned, he oversees file clerks at the Pentagon. In actuality, he is the First Sergeant of SPOOKS, and as such has complete authority in the field, even if a field grade officer is present. He feels he should have died in the Balkans along with his team, but has proven that he is able to bury those feelings to carry out his mission. In his view he has seen the worst, so nothing fazes him, nothing scares him. He can find the positives in the bleakest situations. Taciturn and terse, when he does speak, the words ring with profound authority.

"I got straight "A"s in school and read Julius Caesar's "History of the Gallic Wars" in the fifth grade. This was frowned on in the 'hood as "sucking up to the man," and resulted in severe beatings- until I got my size. I don't let ignorant people tell me what's cool."

SCRIBBLES

CODE NAME: Scribbles
REAL NAME: (CLASSIFIED)
AGE:
PLACE OF BIRTH: (CLASSIFIED)
SPECIALTY: Research & Development
RANK: (CLASSIFIED)

Legend has it that Scribbles had mastered advanced calculus at age three. He had earned a degree from M.I.T. by the time he was thirteen, and he could have been well on his way to being the next Bill Gates if his father, a District Attorney hadn't gone after the Dread Warlock Lucien on a racketeering charge and died a horrible death afflicted by boils and tormented by hordes of locusts. Unable to find any physical and rational cause for these horrors, Scribbles set out to find out for himself and inadvertently stumbled across a SPOOKS investigation. After being recruited by Gunny Biggs and vetted by The Chief, it was revealed to Scribbles that the Warlock had cast the fatal spell on his father. He was instrumental in helping SPOOKS track Lucien to his hidden lair, where the Warlock was finally defeated and captured. Scribbles has been on the team ever since.

Scribbles heads the SPOOKS Research and Development division and creates or supervises all the weapons systems, detection devices and defensive gear used by the field teams. He is physically disorganized, but mentally meticulous. His brain is functioning faster than he can form the words to express his thoughts, so that his speech can seem more like an expression of chaos theory than linear conversation. Yet he always manages to bring the scattered trains of thought back into the station.

"What we call magic may simply be the ability to harness the power of dark matter - the vampire's genetic structure can reproduce internally - so the witch is actually a sidestep in evolution - involuntary twitching in werewolves is a byproduct of muscle expansion during transformation - does anybody have a spare ham sandwich?"

CHET

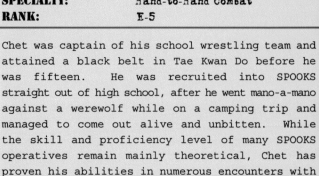

CODE NAME: None

REAL NAME: Chet McQuarrie

AGE: 21

PLACE OF BIRTH:

SPECIALTY: Hand-to-Hand Combat

RANK: E-5

Chet was captain of his school wrestling team and attained a black belt in Tae Kwan Do before he was fifteen. He was recruited into SPOOKS straight out of high school, after he went mano-a-mano against a werewolf while on a camping trip and managed to come out alive and unbitten. While the skill and proficiency level of many SPOOKS operatives remain mainly theoretical, Chet has proven his abilities in numerous encounters with monstrous beings and their minions, leading to his rapid rise up through the ranks of the SPOOKS regular infantry formations all the way up to the Primary Special Operations Team headed by First Sergeant Gunny Biggs.

He is the youngest member of the field team, and is considered a hot-head by Biggs, but has oddly become a sort of "teacher's pet" to The Chief. Everybody, including Gunny Biggs can expect to get a blistering dressing down from the Chief now and then, but the Chief only has smiles and words of praise for Chet. Despite his subordinate rank, Chet is not above rubbing it in at the slightest provocation. Sgt. Biggs has said openly, "It's unbecoming, and disgusting."

Cocky, arrogant, mischievous, stubborn, and reckless, it would seem that Chet is a poor choice for a covert operations field team, but when the chips are down, he always performs, and his loyalty is unquestionable.

"I'm going to run this outfit some day because I've got the moves, and I am just too slick for my own good. No doubt about it."

MURDER, KIDNAPPING, SMUGGLING

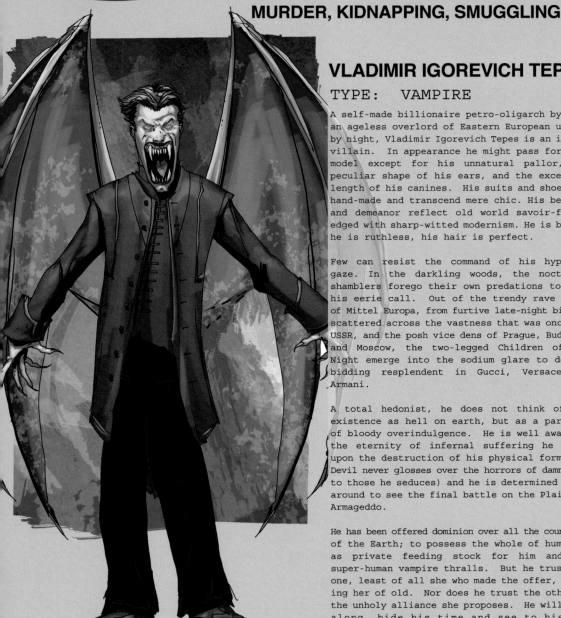

VLADIMIR IGOREVICH TEPES

TYPE: VAMPIRE

A self-made billionaire petro-oligarch by day, an ageless overlord of Eastern European undead by night, Vladimir Igorevich Tepes is an iconic villain. In appearance he might pass for a GQ model except for his unnatural pallor, the peculiar shape of his ears, and the excessive length of his canines. His suits and shoes are hand-made and transcend mere chic. His bearing and demeanor reflect old world savoir-faire, edged with sharp-witted modernism. He is blunt, he is ruthless, his hair is perfect.

Few can resist the command of his hypnotic gaze. In the darkling woods, the nocturnal shamblers forego their own predations to heed his eerie call. Out of the trendy rave clubs of Mittel Europa, from furtive late-night bistros scattered across the vastness that was once the USSR, and the posh vice dens of Prague, Budapest and Moscow, the two-legged Children of the Night emerge into the sodium glare to do his bidding resplendent in Gucci, Versace and Armani.

A total hedonist, he does not think of his existence as hell on earth, but as a paradise of bloody overindulgence. He is well aware of the eternity of infernal suffering he faces upon the destruction of his physical form (the Devil never glosses over the horrors of damnation to those he seduces) and he is determined to be around to see the final battle on the Plains of Armageddo.

He has been offered dominion over all the countries of the Earth; to possess the whole of humanity as private feeding stock for him and his super-human vampire thralls. But he trusts no one, least of all she who made the offer, knowing her of old. Nor does he trust the other in the unholy alliance she proposes. He will play along, bide his time and see to his own interests first.

"I don't drink… Chablis."

CONSIDERED ARMED AND EXTREMELY DANGEROUS AND AN ESCAPE RISK

MURDER, DESTRUCTION OF PRIVATE PROPERTY, ASSAULT WITH INTENT TO KILL, MANSLAUGHTER

JOHANN SUMNER

TYPE: WEREWOLF

He is consumed by a burning hatred for humans, who have been hunting down and killing his kind since the Stone Age. Driven to the fringes of the civilized world, or prowling blighted urban slums in the dead of night, scattered packs of werewolves thirst for revenge as they prey upon the cast-offs of society.

In his untransformed state, he is of average height and build. Dressed in a plain grey suit, he could easily blend into any crowd of commuters in any big city. But in his werewolf state, he stands over 7 feet tall, covered with bristling fur, with yellow glowing eyes, teeth like rows of knives and massive claws tipping elongated sinewy fingers. Even in his seemingly human state the rage is clearly visible in his eyes and in waves of insane psychic energy radiating from his head like heat distortion above a hot pavement. But in his werewolf state, the anger is completely unbound, his rangy muscles vibrating, the fur standing spiky on his back, slobber foaming at the corners of his terrible mouth—and his howl is a thing to freeze the blood, evoking genetic memories of awful things that hunt in darkness...

His natural animosity towards mankind and his propensity towards violence made him a perfect addition to the Witch's unholy alliance. However, he is not particularly loyal to the Witch. Like the Vampire, he has his own agenda, but he has no Machiavellian strategy nor the intellect to create one; he is completely motivated by animal rage and bloodlust.

"Men without their tools and weapons are puny little wretches, only fit to be prey for stronger beings. This is the way it was before. This is the way it will be again."

ONSIDERED ARMED AND EXTREMELY DANGEROUS

MURDER, GRAVEROBBING, EXTORTION, SPELLCASTING

PATIENCE VAN ANDERS

TYPE: WITCH

She is known in certain circles as Patience Van Anders, a fabulously wealthy heiress of multiple fashion and cosmetics dynasties. It has long been rumored that her seemingly perpetual youth is due to Necromancy and a pact with Eternal Darkness. Others say that she is the actual Witch of Endor who was ancient even in the time of King Saul. Whatever the truth may be, it is plain that she is possessed of fantastical magic powers, as well as immense worldly wealth and influence.

The Witch is the real manipulator behind the plot to wrest power from humanity. She knows that as potent as her magic is, she needs the armies of the night that the Vampire and the Werewolf are capable of raising, if she is to keep SPOOKS at bay while she works the spell that will raise legions of zombies to do her bidding. Pity and decency have no meaning to her, and the alliance she proposes will be honored only as long as it serves her purposes.

Svelte, sleek and serpentine, all eyes turn to stare when she glides into exclusive restaurants and the watering spots of the glitterati, clad in shimmering gowns personally designed and crafted for her alone by the top couturiers of Paris, Milan and Tokyo. She is attended by a small army of cold-eyed beautiful young men, who snap to fulfill her smallest whim when they are not nuzzling her perfect ankles like cats in heat.

"They tried to wipe out my kind with the stake and the noose. I shall take their campaign of terror and turn it back upon them with legions of the dead!"

CONSIDERED ARMED AND EXTREMELY DANGEROUS

MURDER, ARSON

HEADLESS JACK

TYPE: UNKNOWN

Confederate General James Zachariah Montague was a cavalry raider second only to the notorious Quantrell for sheer ruthlessness and savagery. During the American Civil War, his depredations left a swath of burnt farms and weeping widows across three states. "Heartless Jack" as he was then called, was leading a mounted troop on the right wing of the final Confederate assault on Pittsburg Landing in Tennessee, when a 10 pound solid shot from a Parrot rifle took his head clean off. He was last seen riding into the cannon smoke, swinging his saber, apparently heedless of his own decapitation. His body was never found...

...Until the Witch brought his tortured being back into the corporeal plane to ride again, although she was unable to reconstitute his head. Ever ironic, the Witch provided him with a substitute Jack-O-Lantern head, which can also be utilized as an incendiary grenade. HEADLESS JACK now leads The Witch's army of the undead.

ONSIDERED ARMED AND EXTREMELY DANGEROUS

MURDER

ZERGUNHEIM

TYPE: GOLEM

Zergunheim is one of a series of flesh automatons created by a renegade Warsaw Pact scientist during the Cold War of the 1950's. The creature is essentially an integrated system of mutated biological parts grown in remote laboratories, and held together by a stainless steel armature powered by miniature electric motors and micro-hydraulics. His huge size is a result of Eastern Bloc miniaturization technology, which remained behind the curve. Zergunheim's original head actually contained vacuum tubes and was topped off with cooling fins. None of this outmoded technology would have actually worked if the inventor had not made a pact with certain Romanian political prisoners. These men were, in fact, sorcerers, and provided potent spells needed to accomplish genuine reanimation.

The six prototypes were intended to be mass-produced as super-soldiers until excessive costs killed the entire project. When that occurred, they were chained and sealed in a hidden fallout shelter, until they were unearthed and sold to the Vampire two decades later.

An automaton's limited intellect makes him a perfect tool for the Vampire. Much of Zergenheim's mental capacity is utilized simply just to walk straight and smash things, and this means he doesn't have any real capacity for treachery. The vampires need guards to watch over their coffins during the day when they are essentially helpless, and the flesh golems are perfect for that job.

Zergunheim, as the biggest and strongest of the creatures, has become the Vampire's personal bodyguard.

ONSIDERED ARMED AND EXTREMELY DANGEROUS

MASS MURDER, TORTURE, NECROMANCY

LUCIEN

TYPE: WARLOCK

The Dread Warlock Lucien has unleashed many deadly plagues and other horrors upon mankind since the dawn of recorded history. Considered to be the most powerful Warlock since Merlin himself. Lucien's base of operations is an underground obsidian tower located beneath a hollow volcano, which sits perched on the edge of a sea of magma. From this hellish lair he hatched his diabolical plots and schemes to wrest control of the Earth from humanity.

Over the centuries, he has taken many apprentices who went on to become powerful witches and warlocks in their own right. His most recent was the seductive Patience Van Anders. It is said that their relationship went beyond that of strictly student and teacher.

Thanks to the efforts of SPOOKS, Lucien was finally tracked to his molten fortress where a massive battle ensued. During this struggle, the top SPOOKS field agent Frank (CLASSIFIED) sustained injuries to his body and soul, and only through supreme effort was able to capture the powerful warlock. It is said these injuries forced him to choose retirement or a desk job. Frank elected for the latter, and was eventually 'promoted' to Commander of the entire organization. Lucien sustained injuries as well, losing one of his eyes, and almost losing the other. Due to his magical nature, he can still 'see' out of his remaining eye, although it is not technically attached to his cerebral cortex.

Lucien is currently held prisoner in a top-secret facility designed to contain the most diabolical supernatural threats known to man.

"I don't have a soul, I have a black cinder, hard as a diamond, cold as a November morning- but it will glow red again... in HELL."

ONSIDERED ARMED AND EXTREMELY DANGEROUS

GHOSTS

by **Geno Salvatore**   Illustrations by **Adam Archer**

The cold February rain whipped about in the gusting wind. The howl of the gale was broken only by the creaking of the old barn, its warped wood bending and straining to hold back the downpour; or perhaps it was something beneath the wood, an unearthly moan drifting out through the cracks to be carried off by the wind and forgotten.

A single light illuminated the dark field, but the flashlight barely dented the smothering darkness. The solitary figure stood tall, his back straight and his head high, staring through the darkness at the ancient structure. The icy rain pelted his bare face, freezing on his cheeks and forming tiny icicles on his moustache. His skin had long since gone numb, and much longer out here would surely mean frostbite.

But the cold Frank felt in his bones this night was not the rain.

He had seen the bodies scattered about the farm: a cat, a chicken, and now a sheep, each left to lie where it had fallen. The farmers were unwilling to touch the corpses, unsure whether the disease would be transmitted to those handling the bodies.

A disease, they thought it. But it was much worse than that, Frank knew. The bodies had their throats ripped open, their blood drained. Drank. Consumed by the vampire growing in their own household. Consumed by the farmers' own fourteen-year-old son.

Frank stared down at the dead sheep at his feet. Unlike the previous two victims, whose blood had been drained without mess, with hardly a trace, this time the blood was everywhere. The sheep's fleece and the snow beneath it were stained a dark red. But that was washing off now in the rain.

The blood was washing off, Frank knew, but only superficially. There would be more blood, this night, and the stains of human blood would be ever more difficult to be rid of.

The mess revealed something to Frank's keen eyes. The vampire was realizing that animals would not sate it, could not nourish it. The blood-craze was growing too great; the vampire was growing desperate. He would have to feast on a human, or perish. He had been resisting the urge with all his soul for so long. But Frank had seen this before, and he knew the inevitable result.

A vampire has no soul.

Frank closed his eyes, trying to remember the pictures, the photographs the teen's beleaguered parents had shown him. He tried to see that image, that sandy-haired youth smiling so brightly. That image he would treasure as he did his duty.

Many of Frank's colleagues refused to see pictures of the victim. They would find it difficult to destroy the turned–be it vampire, werewolf, or otherwise–knowing the person who had once occupied the body. It was much simpler to fight the evil in the abstract.

But Frank knew the truth: that, even if the human was still there, buried beneath the monster, even if his actions were ending a human life, it was still mercy. Frank would destroy this vampire, and he would do it not for the potential victims, not for those that he would kill. Frank would kill the vampire for that smiling teen.

The boy had not killed anyone. He had not suffered the pain and regret and guilt of murder. But, left alone, he surely would, and that evil Frank could not allow.

Frank would save the boy.

The wooden door groaned in protest as Frank pulled it open. A cloud of rust from the old hinges drifted down into the beam of his flashlight, tinting the air red-brown. Inside nothing moved, nothing obvious at least–the vampire was hiding, or it had fled. Frank desperately hoped for the first. Tracking it out in this downpour, in this darkness, would be no easy feat.

Of course, Frank's colleagues were nearby in a van equipped with sensors that would detect the movement of the undead; if the young vampire moved, they would know about it. Or at least, they should know about it, but Frank expected the attention of those two would be turned elsewhere. If they lost the vampire to negligence, Frank would give them an earful; if the escaped vampire then killed someone, he'd give them a hell of a lot more than that.

Frank shook his head; those conversations were for another time.

A crash and a hiss from the hayloft snapped Frank back to his senses.

"Joey?" he called in the closest tone he could manage to 'friendly'.

"Go away," came the response from above, harsh and angry. And scared, Frank knew.

"I'm here to help you, Joey," Frank called up again. "Come to the ladder, let me see you."

"No one can help me," the boy replied, but he did appear at the top of the ladder. He moved as if to climb down, but stopped when he saw Frank.

"It's okay, you can come down, I won't hurt you," Frank said, but the boy didn't react. He just stood there, staring, apparently deep in thought. "I'm from . . ."

"Are you Francis?"

Frank stood up straight as if he'd been struck–and indeed he felt as if he'd been slapped across the face. No one called him Francis, not anymore, not since . . .

"My name is Frank, and I'm from . . ."

Again the boy cut him off. "I'm supposed to wait here for Francis. Go away." The boy turned away, turned to move back into his hayloft.

"I am Francis." He nearly choked on the word. "But please, call me Frank."

The boy turned back to Frank, slowly, and moved directly into the beam of light. "I have a message for you."

"From whom?"

"From him." He tilted his head slightly to reveal his wound, two perfect puncture marks on his neck, bright red against his pale skin and clearly visible even from this distance.

The wind picked up in the background, as did the creaking of the old barn; or per- haps Frank was suddenly more aware of his surroundings. His adrenaline was up, as were the hairs on the back of his neck. The boy took a step forward, then another, then started down the ladder.

Frank held the beam of light steady on the boy with his left hand and fingered his pistol with his right. A bullet wouldn't hurt a full vampire, but the boy hadn't yet feasted on human blood–he hadn't yet fully turned. One shot, right in the head, and the youthful creature would stop. Of course, Frank would have to stake its heart to complete the kill or it would simply wake up again, but an unmoving target is much easier to stab than one fighting back.

Soon the boy was on the ground, barely five feet in front of Frank. The boy stared at him, and Frank noted there was still light in his blue eyes, still a spark of life. A good sign.

"So what's this message, Joey?" Frank asked.

"He says to tell you, the end is near."

"The end is near? That's it?"

"Don't interrupt me!" The force of his– its–voice knocked Frank back a step; the sudden realization that he'd let a vampire get so close to him pushed him back a few more. His pistol was out of its holster in a blink and pointed straight at the boy who suddenly looked so much less the boy and more the monster.

The vampire bared its teeth–its fangs were fully developed, Frank noted–but it did not advance. Its voice dropped an octave, a deep booming baritone so out of place coming from this teen barely out of puberty, this hundred-pound youth. "The end is near, and he will show it to you. There is a boathouse thirty miles from here, on the Nashua River. No roads. No people. Just trees. Go there tomorrow night, and go alone. That is the message."

As he finished, Joey took a step back, and he seemed to shrink. He closed his mouth, blinked a few times, then looked back up at Frank. That tiny spark of life was there again, along with something else–tears.

"You came to help me, right?"

"Yes, son, I'm here to help." Frank did not lower his pistol, but took a step forward. Joey did not shy away.

"Is there a cure?"

"No."

Frank fired before the boy could respond. The gale outside seemed to stop, only for a split second, to let the shot ring out across the fields to the farmhouses nearby, to the boy's poor parents, and his siblings, and neighbors, and whoever else might be listening. The wind paused until the echoes died, then began again with renewed fury.

Frank moved to the fallen boy, shone his flashlight down upon him as he had with the dead sheep outside. A single bullet hole, perfectly placed, center of his forehead. The eyes shut tight, as if he knew it was coming and didn't want to see it. A pool of blood forming beneath it, black as the night outside.

Frank knelt beside the teen and put his hand on the cold skin of his face. He ran his fingers over every inch of it, memorizing it, forming a tactile picture to match the visual one already in his memory. He would hold on to every bit of this boy that he could, like all the other victims. Another one saved, he thought. Another ghost to follow him around.

Better that than the alternative, though. The boy died before he could make any ghosts of his own.

Frank reached to his belt and pulled out the wooden stake, and slowly, carefully, lovingly moved its point to the hollow of Joey's chest.

Frank banged on the rear door of the surveillance van, not hard but hard enough to be heard. The quiet rhythmic noise within the vehicle stopped, to be replaced a moment later by the uneven clatter of surprised scrambling as the two occupants hurried to right themselves.

The door cracked open, the light inside the van spilling out into the night, cutting through the gloom and the rain, illuminating Frank's sodden features.

"Verify before you open, kid," Frank said as he pulled himself into the van, pushing past the younger man, Anthony, one of his underlings on this mission. Frank was more than content to ignore him, and Anthony in turn was happy to be ignored–it gave him time to tuck his shirt back in, to adjust his belt.

Toward the front of the van sat the other member of the team, Michelle, a young woman about Anthony's age. She had her back turned to Frank, staring intently at the panel of monitors in front of her–and, Frank knew, discreetly buttoning up her blouse. They had played through this scenario three times already, at each of the previous stops along the trail of victims left by their vampire.

"Nothing on the scopes all night, boss," she said.

Like you would know, Frank mused. These two had probably watched those scopes for all of ten minutes after he'd headed for the old barn.

But then again, so far the expensive instruments had been all but useless. The undead emitted a different sort of energy than living beings, and these scopes picked up on that aura. But their quarry had never come close enough to be detected. If they had been staring at the monitor all night, all Anthony and Michelle would have seen was Joey's weak aura, sitting in one place for hours, until he died.

Until Frank killed him.

So it was little surprise that, in their boredom, they found another way to occupy the hours.

Or perhaps it wasn't boredom. These

two were greener than green, twenty-somethings recruited fresh out of college, never been in the field before. Neither of them had seen a vampire, or a werewolf or ghost or anything else supernatural. Part of them would surely cling to the notion that it was all fake, that the world was as simple as they'd believed all their young lives.

And besides that, neither of them had seen a kill. For them to watch the scopes, to see Joey's aura simply vanish, would be difficult.

But why were these two greens all the support he had this time? They were dealing with an old vampire, a powerful and intelligent and malicious being, on United States soil. Such activity was rare, if not unheard of, and should have drawn a lot of resources. Why did Frank, their best field agent, get this minimal, nearly useless support for this important mission?

"Frank!" Anthony's hand was on his shoulder, shaking him less-than gently. Frank's own hand shot up to grab Anthony's wrist, instinctively trying to stave off

the assault, before he realized the younger man was just trying to get his attention–had probably been trying to get his attention for the last few minutes.

"What?"

"Where we heading next? What's the plan? Same as before?" Anthony sounded less-than excited at the prospect. Same as before would mean another week of roaming, sweeping with the scopes and monitoring radio traffic, hoping in vain to catch a hint of the vampire's whereabouts before he struck again. But inevitably, they'd find nothing, until a report came in about someone's son or daughter or cousin behaving strangely, and dead animals.

Same as before would mean another victim.

"No." Frank sat down to collect his thoughts. Anthony and Michelle both turned to look at him, to stare at him.

"The kid had a message. From the vampire. He said we have to go to a boathouse thirty miles from here. He said, the end is near."

"That's good," Anthony said. "We can finally get off this shit mission."

"Good?" Michelle cut in before Frank could respond. "The end is near? That doesn't sound ominous to you?"

"Ominous, sure. But I ain't scared of this vampire. We've killed five of them already since we been out here, what, I'm gonna be scared of one more?"

"'We've killed'? You mean Frank's killed."

"Whatever. And Frank will kill this one too and then we can all go home."

They both talked about the kills–the dead kids–so matter-of-factly. So green.

"Enough." Frank's voice wasn't loud, but it was more than enough to shut the other two up. "Get out the maps and find the boathouse. We've got a day, let's make good use of it."

In minutes the maps were spread out on the floor of the van, Anthony and Michelle crouched in front of it, pinpointing their location and looking for possible matches to his description. The maps were thorough and detailed, and these two kids were at least competent enough to deal with this. Frank didn't bother to look at the map–he focused on the faces of his companions.

Michelle hid it well, but to Frank's experienced eye she looked frightened indeed. Her face was paler than usual, her eyes a bit too wide, a bit too dry. Anthony, on the other hand, looked positively giddy. He could hardly sit still, and a hint of a smile kept creeping up the sides of his mouth.

They should be somewhere in the middle, Frank knew. On the one hand, they finally had a lead, a chance to finish the mission. On the other, did they really want it to end on the vampire's terms? They were surely walking into a trap.

Even Frank jumped in surprise at the sudden sharp rap on the rear hatch.

Frank turned to look at the door, to see Anthony moving toward it. Confirm before you open, Frank thought but had no time to say, and suddenly the door was cracked open and darkness seemed to flood in.

No, not darkness. Just one dark object. The barrel of a shotgun.

Suddenly all the air was ringing with noise and filled with blinding light, first the flash of the gun then sparks as the slug struck the sensor unit. Sparks flew, monitors toppled. Anthony fell away, blinded and deafened; Michelle lay on the ground, unmoving. Only Frank saw the door pull open, revealing nothing but the pouring rain and the smothering dark outside.

Frank leapt forward, to the front of the van, into the driver's seat. In one swift motion he turned the vehicle on, threw it into gear, and hit the gas. The ungainly vehicle lurched forward, and all the loose equipment in the rear slid backward, very nearly pushing Anthony out the open hatch.

To his credit, the young man caught his senses quickly, righted himself, and slammed the door shut just as another shot rang out.

In the rear-view mirror Frank saw headlights as another car fired up. He pushed the van as fast as it could go, but the downpour had turned the dirt road into mud and the turns were nearly impossible to navigate with any speed.

"We have incoming. Get a gun." Frank kept his voice calm, perfectly steady, reassuring to his young companions.

"Michelle's down," Anthony called back. Frank saw him move to her side, check her pulse. "She's breathing, but she's bleeding." He moved to the medical locker.

"No time for that now," Frank said, and a shotgun blast from the tailing car accentuated his point. "We've got to get these guys off our tail first."

Anthony opened the med locker, apparently ignoring the order. Frank opened his mouth to repeat himself, but the words stuck in his throat.

In the back of the van, a red light flashed and one of the monitors emitted a low buzzing noise.

"Contact," Frank said. "What is it, kid?" His voice was quiet now, barely a whisper.

Anthony apparently had heard the buzz as well. He dropped the armful of supplies he had been gathering, and moved quickly to the scope.

"Undead, strong aura," he said.

"Obviously. Where?"

"I can't tell, the monitor is cracked." The buzz grew louder.

"Getting closer," Frank said.

"Right on top of us," Anthony answered, a note of fear in his voice for the first time.

Another bang echoed out from the vehicle behind them, a shotgun blast—and then another, different noise, and the headlights stopped in their tracks, as if the car had slammed into a brick wall.

Then the headlights were moving again. Up, up they went, then away, flying off the side of the road, crashing into a tree several yards off the ground.

Frank jammed the brakes, the van skidding to a stop. He leapt out of his seat and rushed to the arms locker, throwing it open and reaching for two of the assault rifles. He tossed one to Anthony, took up the other and moved to the rear hatch. He clicked on the attached flashlight as he kicked open the door and hopped out into the deluge.

Frank took three steps into the night before he realized Anthony wasn't following.

"It's him! It's the vampire!" Anthony said—screamed—to Frank.

"No shit, it's him. Get up off your ass and let's go kill the sonofabitch."

"We can't leave Michelle here, she's bleeding."

Make your excuses, kid. "Keep your eyes open, at least. I'll be back." So green.

Frank strode out toward the wrecked car. He couldn't see an inch outside the narrow beam of his flashlight. He was essentially blind, but he didn't care. He knew the vampire wouldn't still be out here. The creature had an agenda of its own, and it wouldn't jeopardize that agenda by confronting Frank here and now. Frank walked through the darkness for a different reason.

He had only one point of reference in his march, and he made straight for it. A minute later, he saw the twisted wreck of an old pickup. Rusted and beaten before, now the thing was utterly trashed, wrapped around a tree sidelong. The driver was still inside, covered in blood, obviously dead even from this range.

He was covered in blood, but Frank knew his face immediately anyway. Joey's father.

Frank moved to the wreck, put his hand on the man's face, closed his eyes. Another face to remember, another ghost.

But no sign of the vampire.

When Frank returned to the van, he found Michelle still lying down, but moving at least. Her head was wrapped in a bandage and she was holding an ice pack to her forehead. Anthony was again crouched beside the map.

———

It's the perfect spot for an ambush."

He wasn't wrong. The boathouse was a mile from any paved road, building, or other sign of human life. It was flush against the river, which was swollen from the melting snow and the previous night's rain. Hills rose steeply on all sides—even the one dirt road leading away from the place ascended at an angle almost too steep to climb. The whole area was densely wooded, thick with underbrush. The river was not wide, perhaps forty feet across, but the current was strong and the detritus of the early thaw rushed past. The far bank looked much like this one, a steep hill covered in trees.

The boathouse itself was a dilapidated old wooden structure that looked as if it would soon fall down of its own accord. Inside there were racks sufficient to hold perhaps a dozen shells, but the all stood empty. The door was warped, the hinges bent, and it would not shut. Debris covered the floor, though the area immediately behind the door was mostly clear except for a small circle of stones filled with ash–the remnants of a crude campfire.

"Yeah, I can buy that," Frank said. The vampire had told him to come alone, but Frank knew better than that. Of course, the vampire surely would know that Frank wouldn't be so foolish, too.

He took a quick survey of the layout. Frank would have to be inside, to draw the vampire out; Anthony would have to be somewhere he could see into the boathouse. With the only door facing the river, the best vantage point would be on the opposite bank. Which was fine, since that was the heaviest cover anyway.

"You set up over there with a rifle. I'll stay here. Wait until he lands, then shoot for the head." Frank nodded to himself as he formulated his plan.

Anthony looked somewhat less sure. "Kind of obvious, don't you think?"

"Absolutely, but this bastard will be too cocky to care."

"Because bullets can't hurt him."

"Exactly." Frank nearly laughed at the sour expression on Anthony's face.

"So I'm going to shoot him. In the head. With bullets that can't hurt him."

"Yeah."

"And then what?"

Frank just smiled and started to walk back the way they'd come, back toward the van.

All Frank wanted from Anthony was a distraction. Killing a vampire would be no easy task–he'd have to stake the undead thing in the heart, at night, with it unrestrained. Not a promising prospect. But if Anthony shot it a few times, got it to turn around, then he might have a chance.

One single chance. And if he missed, he was dead.

They were all dead.

Frank turned to his green companion. "If it comes after you, jump in the river."

"Brilliant plan. Freeze to death before it can get me. Yeah."

"We'll set the van a couple miles downriver. Michelle can fish you out. A little hypothermia is better than a lot of blood loss, any day." Never mind that the vampire would just follow him, if it wanted to; never mind that Michelle was barely strong enough to stand right now, let alone pull him from an icy river. The last thing they could afford now was low morale.

Besides, the vampire was looking for him, for Frank. Maybe it would ignore the others after it was done with him.

Anthony started to respond, but a burst of static from the radio on Frank's belt cut him off. The static formed into a voice–Michelle's voice.

"Guys, the scope's going haywire," she said. "Something's coming. Aren't vampires supposed to be like, allergic to light?"

Yes, they are, Frank thought. He and Anthony locked eyes for a moment, then sprinted off down the dirt path.

———

The van was empty.

No blood, no sign of a struggle, no Michelle. Just empty. Anthony spent the next few minutes in a frenzy of motion, whirling about the empty vehicle looking for any hint, any sign of Michelle, tracks or blood or anything. Frank just stood there. There was no sign to be found, he already knew. She was gone, and they wouldn't get her back.

As Anthony spun past Frank for the tenth time that minute, he put out his hand to grab the younger man on the shoulder, to stop him. Anthony responded with a thrown punch; Frank didn't even flinch. He took the hit square in the jaw, staggered back a step.

He deserved that swing, Frank thought.

Anthony did not advance. He just stared. Frank wished he would charge in swinging. The stare hurt more than the punch.

"We shouldn't have left her alone."

"No shit."

"We should have seen it coming."

"Shut it." Anthony had given up on finding a clue here, but he hadn't given up on moving; he paced around in a circle. "We need to do something. We need to call for backup."

"There's no backup within two hundred miles," Frank said. "We're on our own." Why is that, he wondered, almost said it aloud. Why were they left alone, to fend for themselves? Two green kids–now one– and one aging field agent. That wouldn't be sufficient for a job like this, and the people in charge would know it. Or should know it, at least.

Did they expect Frank's team to fail? Did they want it? This had been no mistake, no misallocation of resources–they'd been out here for over a month, trying to pick up the vampire's trail. The vampire had been here even longer, taking his individual victims and waiting for . . . whatever it is a vampire waits for.

Waiting for me, Frank thought.

Before last night, before the message, the trail had been ice cold; the vampire never stuck its neck out until it understood what was pursuing it. If a larger team had been sent, perhaps it never would have shown itself at all.

The word "bait" flashed through Frank's mind.

Frank rushed past Anthony and straight into the van, headed for the radio unit. He flicked it on, took the receiver, sent out a call.

"Spooks, come in, this is Red Dog." No answer.

"Spooks HQ, come in, this is Red Dog, request assistance." Static.

"Spooks assets, if you can hear this, this is Frank. We need assistance. We'll be at the old boathouse, Groton woods, Nashua river, tonight. If you can be there, please do." The radio crackled to life.

"So you'll still be coming, Francis?" The voice on the other end was low, deep but somehow grating, unearthly. "I expected no less. You won't run away tail between your legs."

"I won't run at all, not from a coward like you," Frank snarled back.

The vampire laughed. "Just setting the field, my young friend. These things are so much more interesting when there's more on the line than just killing each other."

"I will kill you."

"I have no doubt."

Frank dropped the receiver and moved for the door. The vampire's voice crackled across the speaker one last time, loudly.

"Hey Red Dog, bring the kid this time. See you tonight, brother."

————

Night brought another storm with it. This time it was snow. Giant snowflakes drifting, blowing in the gusty wind, obscuring everything in a veil of white.

Frank and Anthony stood side-by-side in the boathouse, near the back to shelter themselves from the biting cold. Each held an assault rifle, an old Kalashnikov, crude but still powerfully functional. But those would be useless against their foe tonight, they knew.

Anthony hadn't spoken a word to Frank since they left the van. The harshest, most hateful anger simmered behind his eyes. For his part, Frank gave the youth his space. His own pain was no less than Anthony's; he blamed himself for losing Michelle. But trying to enunciate that would be pointless.

They could talk later. Right now, they had a job to finish.

For hours they waited, unmoving, silent. At midnight, their vigil ended; the vampire walked in through the front door, appearing as if from nowhere, as if he had been part of the darkness.

And he did not come alone. In front of him he held Michelle. She was walking of her own power, but barely, staggering and looking more than a little drunk. Anthony seemed elated to see her, happy that she was alive; Frank knew better, knew the signs.

The vampire stopped. "Welcome to my humble home, Francis. It's been oh so long since we last met."

"Don't play that game. We've never met."

"Oh ho, is that so? I was a guest in your house once, and I felt I should return the favor."

Frank stared long and hard at the vampire, knowing perfectly well what it was insinuating. But after a moment he was sure of it: this was not the vampire that had killed his family.

Would it matter if it were, he wondered. Would he somehow give more, more effort, more of himself, more willingness to die, if he were facing that horrible being?

It was a question for another day. Right now, he had to face the problem before him. The plan was set, the ball was in

play. But judging by the way Anthony was twitching, the plan wouldn't last long.

Frank had to take control. "Hiding behind a human shield? Again you act the coward."

"Human shield? Well, not in the strictest sense, no." The vampire roughly took Michelle by the hair, pulling her head to the side, revealing the fresh blood staining her neck and blouse, the open puncture wounds on her throat.

Frank started to answer, but Anthony reacted first. A burst of fire rang out from his rifle, one-two-three, perfect shots right over Michelle's shoulder, right into the vampire's grinning face. The thing barely flinched, but Anthony strode forward firing again, perfect again. He mumbled something unintelligible as he moved. He's completely unconscious, Frank thought. And a good thing for it; another burst rang out, again three shots, dead in the vampire's face.

Anthony's gun barrel very nearly reached the vampire before the thing finally reacted. It dropped Michelle unceremoniously to the side and leapt forward, blindingly fast, grabbing the young man by the throat and lifting him clear off the ground.

Anthony hardly seemed to care; he used his rifle like a club, smashing the vampire across the mouth once, twice, thrice in succession. He was aiming for the fangs, Frank knew somehow. He wanted to break the fangs. Frank scrambled forward to grab the fallen Michelle and pull her out of the way.

The vampire paid him no heed, focused as he was on the fiery young man in his hand. He said nothing, did nothing, just stood there smiling as Anthony vented his fury.

He is cocky, Frank thought. But not so confident. He has to show his strength. He wants us to fear him, to fear his power.

Anthony stopped suddenly, looking confused. His rifle dropped to the floor; his hand shot up to his throat, to the undead hand holding his throat, blocking his airway.

"Ah, yet another weakness of humanity. You are so dependant on your precious air." The vampire was mocking him, laughing at him, but not paying attention to him; it didn't notice that Anthony tried to fend it off with only one hand.

The other hand reached for his belt, for the stake strapped there.

He stabbed out, struck the vampire dead in the chest. But too high, not in the heart. He tried to withdraw, to strike again, but the vampire was too fast, and suddenly too angry. It turned and threw him, hard, through one of the boat racks, through the wall behind it, out into the storm.

Frank winced at the sight, at Anthony's flight. But he had more pressing matters to attend as the vampire turned and stalked toward him.

It was pissed now, angry and probably scared. It had been staked by a human; it had nearly died—a truly frightening prospect to a creature that fancied itself immortal.

It did not slow as its foot brushed aside the stones surrounding the old campfire. It did not hesitate when Frank held his hand up before his face, holding a small metal object. It did not notice the red light in the ash at its feet as the detonator on the explosive charge hidden in the ash picked up the signal.

It noticed when the charge blew up.

The vampire flew forward, flipped over midair, and slammed hard into the wall barely four feet from Frank, upside down and clearly injured. Frank was partially blinded, partially deafened, finding his breath hard to come by. But he did not, could not, hesitate; he grabbed a stake from his belt and dived at the fallen creature. It tried to fend him off, but it too was blind and at an awkward angle and it couldn't get its arms into any sort of defensive position.

Frank rushed in, the stake rushed in, deadly accurate, right beside the stake still sticking from the vampire's chest. His aim was perfect.

The vampire grabbed his arm, but there was no strength in its grip; it looked into his eyes, but could not see. It tried to open its mouth but could find no words. It died.

Frank knelt there a long time, staring at his fallen foe. The plan had worked, the vampire was dead–already its flesh began to decompose, catching up on centuries of rotting it should have done–but the cost had been high. And it would only get higher, he knew, looking at Michelle.

She sat slumped against the wall, unconscious or barely conscious. Her head tilted to the side, showing her wound, showing her neck and shoulder caked in dried blood. Her face was ashen, pale except a single trickle of red blood running from the side of her mouth down her cheek, drip-dripping into a small pool on the ground.

She is already dead, Frank reminded himself. He took a stake from the vampire's chest–Anthony's stake; he felt it would be more fitting–and slowly rose.

He knelt beside her, put his hand gently on her cheek, turned her to face him. He stared into her eyes, perfect green eyes, so young and full of life just days ago, now empty and sunken. The spark was still there; when she woke up, she would remember herself yet. But that would not last. Soon she would be like the wretched corpse beside her, a bloodthirsty monster. He could not allow that.

For her sake, he would kill her. He would save her.

Frank brought the stake gently to her chest.

The click of a pistol cocking at his ear stopped him.

"Put it down, Frank," Anthony said. Tough kid. He should be dead.

"She's already gone," he said. "Let her go."

"No, no, no, we can't kill her. We can't. We'll figure something out, take her to HQ, they'll know what to do."

"They'll just kill her. We shouldn't make her suffer that long."

"Screw you. If they won't help her, I will. I'll take her away, hide her away from everyone where she can't hurt anyone."

"She'll just kill you. Do you want her to have to live with that?"

"She won't!" Anthony was screaming now. Denial is such an ugly thing to witness, Frank thought. But he could surely sympathize with the pain this young man felt.

"She wouldn't, Michelle wouldn't. But this isn't Michelle any longer." Frank rose as he spoke, turning slowly to face Anthony.

The younger man struggled to find an answer, any answer, some valid reason to stop Frank. But none came.

"Let me finish this," Frank said.

"No."

"Then you finish it." He held out the stake; Anthony took it. Frank moved slowly out of his way.

Anthony knelt down before Michelle, as Frank had done a moment earlier. He moved the stake toward her chest; his hands were shaking, trembling uncontrollably. His eyes never left hers. He pulled back for the killing stroke and . . .

Stood.

"I won't do it," he said, turning to face Frank–turning to point his pistol at Frank again. "There's another way."

"No there is not. Don't be a fool, kid."

"There is. I'll let her turn me." Frank lost his breath at the assertion.

"Turn you? You'll damn yourself, damn

both of you!"

"Better damned for eternity with her than alive without her," Anthony growled. "You gonna leave, or do I have to shoot you?"

"I'm not leaving," Frank said. "But you don't have to shoot anyone. Just stop and think about what you're doing."

"I have thought about it." He thumbed back the hammer, put his finger on the trigger.

Frank looked into his eyes, and what he saw there truly frightened him. Anthony had indeed thought about it; his mind was not going to change. He meant to pull that trigger.

Frank leapt forward just as the gunshot sounded. A line of fire creased Frank's temple, a searing cut left by the passing bullet, quickly cooled by the flow of blood. The pain would have stopped a lesser man, but Frank just drove forward, crashing hard into Anthony's chest, knocking them both off their feet.

They rolled and thrashed about, finally coming to rest with Anthony on top, pistol still in one hand, Frank's hair in the other. He tried to bring the pistol about, to put it against Frank's forehead and fire, but he stopped suddenly.

He stopped, and he jerked, against the object now lodged in his chest, the stake he had dropped and somehow Frank had grabbed, and even more amazingly had driven through his breastbone and into his heart.

Anthony tried to bring the gun about, tried to shoot this man who had killed him. But there was no strength left in his arm.

Frank reached up, cradled Anthony's head in his hand, brought him close. "You can have your eternity with her," he whispered. "You can have eternity in a far better place than this. My friend."

Anthony pulled his head back; a trickle of blood dripped out of his mouth onto Frank's face. His lips quivered as he formed them into his last words.

"Screw you."

————

Frank walked through the woods, alone, through the blowing wind and the rapidly-piling snow. The conflagration that had been the boathouse burned behind him, but Frank did not look back. Both Kalashnikovs were slung over

his shoulder; in his pockets he had every item, every patch, every weapon that could connect Anthony to SPOOKS. The vampire's body–and Michelle's body–would turn to smoke and ash; the only thing investigators would find was the young man's burnt corpse.

Frank's eyes were barely open, focused instead on the images in his head. Those two kids, just out of college. So green. His hand moved unconsciously, tracing the lines of their faces, first Michelle's then Anthony's, then again, over and over. They would follow him around, like all the others. Two more among the throng of ghosts at his back.

His other hand was in his pocket, clutching firmly another object he had taken from Anthony. A small metal object he could not bear to leave there, to let burn. An engagement ring he had planned to give to Michelle after the mission.

Two more ghosts.

SPOOKS COVER 1A BY GREG STAPLES

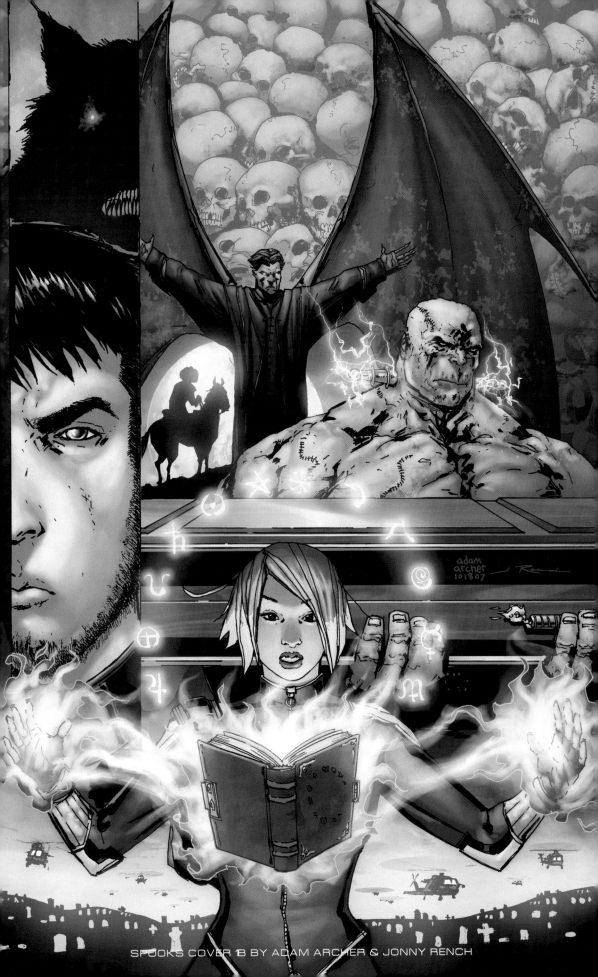

SPOOKS COVER 13 BY ADAM ARCHER & JONNY RENCH

SPOOKS COVER 2A BY FEDERICO DALESSANDRO

SPOOKS COVER 2B BY ADAM ARCHER & JONNY RENCH

SPOOKS COVER 3A BY BILL SIENKIEWICZ

SPOOKS COVER 4A BY ADAM ARCHER & JONNY RENCH

SPOOKS COVER 4B BY DREW STRUZAN

YOU'RE DOING ALL THE TALKING, FISH-CAKES. IT TAKES A HEAP OF MAGIC TO MAKE THE DEAD WALK-- WHERE'S IT COME FROM?

FROM PYRAMID IN PYRAMID...

...THERE!

GUESS WE'RE ALL TAKING A LITTLE *CLIMB*, AMIGOS.

OKAY, YOU LET ME GO NOW?

NOT BY A LONG-SHOT, SCROD-HEAD. I WANT YOU HANDY FOR INSTANT GRATIFICATION IF IT TURNS OUT YOU SOLD US A WOOF-TICKET.

HOW CAN THERE BE A PYRAMID *IN* A PYRAMID? HUH?

WE HAVE TO EXAMINE INTERNALLY--TO PEER AMID.

YOU'RE A WEIRDO, DX.

I'M WEIRD? YOU HAVE A DIGIT FOR A NAME.

SO, *THIS* IS WHAT HE MEANS BY "PYRAMID IN PYRAMID..."

TO BE CONTINUED IN THE PAGES OF SPOOKS: OMEGA TEAM!

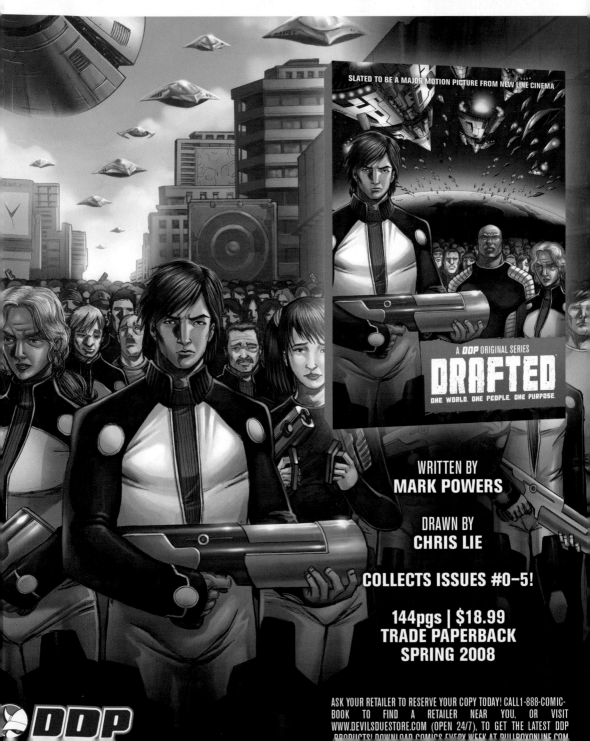